LEGO® Friends

The Sunshine Ranch

PUFFIN

PUFFIN BOOKS

Published by the Penguin Group
Penguin Books Ltd, 80 Strand, London WC2R 0RL, England
Penguin Group (USA) Inc., 375 Hudson Street, New York, New York 10014, USA
Penguin Group (Canada), 90 Eglinton Avenue East, Suite 700, Toronto, Ontario, Canada M4P 2Y3
(a division of Pearson Penguin Canada Inc.)
Penguin Ireland, 25 St Stephen's Green, Dublin 2, Ireland (a division of Penguin Books Ltd)
Penguin Group (Australia), 707 Collins Street, Melbourne, Victoria 3008, Australia
(a division of Pearson Australia Group Pty Ltd)
Penguin Books India Pvt Ltd, 11 Community Centre, Panchsheel Park, New Delhi – 110 017, India
Penguin Group (NZ), 67 Apollo Drive, Rosedale, Auckland 0632, New Zealand
(a division of Pearson New Zealand Ltd)
Penguin Books (South Africa) (Pty) Ltd, Block D, Rosebank Office Park, 181 Jan Smuts Avenue, Parktown
North, Gauteng 2193, South Africa

Penguin Books Ltd, Registered Offices: 80 Strand, London WC2R 0RL, England

puffinbooks.com

First published 2014
001

Written by Poppy Bloom
Illustrations by AMEET Studio Sp. z o.o.
Text and illustrations copyright © AMEET Sp. z o.o., 2014

Produced by AMEET Sp. z o.o. under license from the LEGO Group.

AMEET Sp. z o.o.
Nowe Sady 6, 94-102 Łódź – Poland
ameet@ameet.pl   www.ameet.pl

LEGO, the LEGO logo and the Brick and Knob configurations
are trademarks of the LEGO Group.
©2014 The LEGO Group.

British Library Cataloguing in Publication Data
A CIP catalogue record for this book is available from the British Library

ISBN: 978-1-40939-304-7

Item name: LEGO® Friends. The Sunshine Ranch
Series: LBW
Item number: LBW-103
Batch: 01

The Sunshine Ranch

Poppy Bloom

Andrea
Star Performer

Mia
Animal Lover

Olivia
Brilliant
Inventor

Stephanie
Social Butterfly

Emma
Stylish Designer

Chelsea
Uptown Girl

Jane
Shy Classmate

Contents

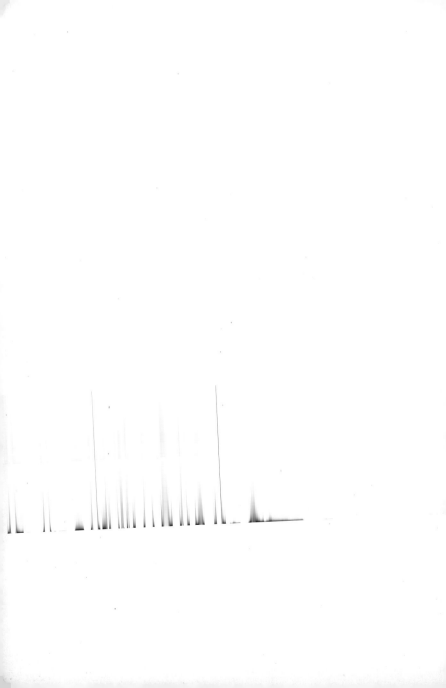

1
Road Trip

Emma pressed her nose to the cool glass of the bus window. Outside, the Heartlake City skyline was getting smaller and smaller as the bus trundled away on the Heartlake Highway. Up ahead, the road curved past the foothills of the Clearspring Mountains. Fields of corn grew on both sides of the road and in the distance Emma could see cattle grazing in some meadows.

"Are we there yet?" Stephanie asked. As she leaned past to peer out of the window, her blonde hair tickled Emma's cheek.

A laugh came from the seat behind Emma
and Stephanie. Their friend Mia's head popped
into view.

"You've asked that at least ten times in the
past fifteen minutes, Steph," Mia teased.

Stephanie shrugged and
tugged playfully on Mia's
long red ponytail.

"I can't help it. The Sunshine Ranch sounds like such an amazing place. I can't wait to get there and start having fun!"

"Me too." Andrea leaned over from the seat across the aisle from Emma and Stephanie.

"Me three." Olivia popped into view beside Mia. "I'm glad the headteacher decided to make it our spring class trip. I've been hearing about the Sunshine Ranch ever since I moved to Heartlake City. But I never knew it belonged to your grandparents until you told us, Mia!"

Olivia was the only one of the five best friends who hadn't been born and raised in Heartlake City. Emma already found it hard to believe that Olivia hadn't lived there forever. She couldn't imagine life without her!

Mia grinned. "Trust me, you guys will love it. I can't believe none of you have ever been there," she said.

"Oooh, tell us something exciting about the ranch, Mia," Andrea said eagerly.

Mia laughed. "Well, I don't know if I should give away too much," she teased, her eyes sparkling. "I will tell you there are lots of animals there, though."

Emma smiled. "Of course you would start with the animals, Mia!" Mia loved animals so much that she wanted to be a vet someday.

"Come on!" Olivia said excitedly. "Give us a few more details!"

"Oh all right – maybe just a few," Mia said. "The ranch has a cool apple orchard and there are lots of horses and other animals living here. My grandparents also have a market stall where you can buy fresh fruit and vegetables on the way out. Oh! And one more thing – they teach people how to ride Western."

"What does that mean?" asked Olivia.

"It's how cowboys ride horses," Mia explained. "They have a special saddle and know how to use the reins with one hand so they can lasso cattle. It's pretty cool."

Andrea's eyes lit up. "Ooh, I've always wanted to try Western riding," she said. "It looks like fun." She patted her curly dark hair. "Plus I look great in cowboy hats!"

"Yeah." Stephanie nudged Emma playfully. "Trying a new riding style is a good excuse to get a whole new wardrobe of riding clothes! Right, Emma?"

Emma glanced down at her outfit and grinned sheepishly. All four of her best friends – and everyone else who knew her – knew that she

loved fashion. She'd chosen her outfit for this trip carefully. She was wearing a ruffled denim skirt, a sparkly pink-and-white shirt and ankle boots. A cute pink bandana held back her long, wavy black hair.

"I just wish I had those adorable pink
sequined cowboy boots I saw at
Deluxo Duds last week,"
she said. "Those would
make my outfit
perfect."

"Don't you mean cowgirl boots?" Andrea corrected.

Emma laughed. "You're right – they were definitely cowgirl boots!"

"I wonder if we'll get to try square dancing today," Olivia said. "I looked at the ranch's website last night, and that was one of the activities they listed."

Andrea looked interested. "I hope so! I've never tried square dancing, but it looks like fun."

"You'll probably be a natural at it, Andrea," Olivia said. "Your last dance recital was great!"

Emma had to agree. Andrea was a natural performer. She was a fantastic singer, as well as being a talented actress, dancer and musician. All of Andrea's friends had gone to watch a performance at her dance studio a few weeks earlier.

"Yeah, you were amazing," Emma said, smiling at Andrea. "I especially loved that sparkly green dress you wore for your last number. It really set off your eyes."

"That was a cute one, wasn't it?" Andrea struck a pose, fluttering her lashes over her bright green eyes. Then her smile faded slightly as a loud laugh came from the back of the bus. "Too bad Chelsea Noble had to be in my group for the recital," she added. "She complained the whole time about not getting all the solos."

Emma glanced behind her. Chelsea was sitting with her friends in the back row. She had wavy blonde hair and brown eyes and was more dressed up than most of the people on the trip in a trendy purple dress with a flouncy skirt.

Mia looked sympathetic. "I know Chelsea can be annoying. She's a pretty good dancer, though."

"I guess everyone has some kind of talent," Stephanie said with a grin.

Emma just nodded. None of the friends got along that well with Chelsea Noble.

Chelsea tended to act snobby and loved to gossip. She was always bragging about her designer wardrobe and her expensive mobile phone.

"Enough about Chelsea," Andrea said. "Since Mia won't tell us anything, what other activities were on the website, Olivia?"

"Lots of stuff!" Olivia started ticking things off on her fingers. "You can pick your own fruit from the orchards, collect eggs from the henhouse, watch the cowboys do roping demonstrations and…"

Emma's attention drifted as her friends continued to discuss the ranch. Her gaze wandered up the aisle to a dark-haired freckly girl sitting all alone near the front. Her name was Jane. She'd moved to Heartlake City just after Christmas and was the new girl at Heartlake High. She was in a couple of Emma's classes, but Emma hadn't talked to her much. Actually, now that she thought about it, Emma realized that she hadn't seen Jane talking to anybody.

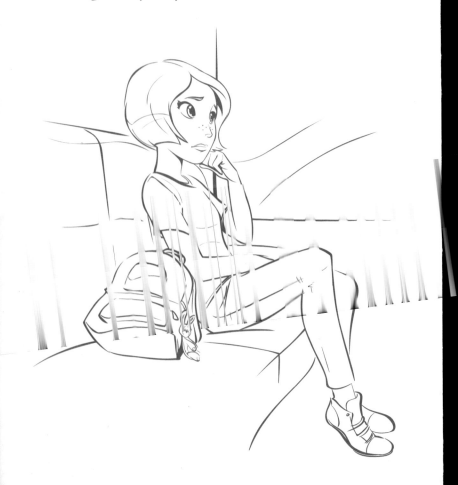

She remembered something else too. Jane always wore clothes in very muted colours. Today she was dressed in black jeans and a dark T-shirt. Emma couldn't imagine being happy without her own colourful wardrobe. For her, one of the best parts of every day was deciding what interesting new outfit to wear.

"Jane seems really shy, doesn't she?" Emma said, interrupting the others' conversation.

"Huh?" Mia turned to look at Emma. "You mean the new girl?"

Emma nodded. "It doesn't seem like she's making friends at school," she said. "She never talks to anyone and she's always alone."

"Yeah," Andrea agreed. "I said hi to her in the hall yesterday and she didn't even answer. She just sort of smiled and then rushed away."

Stephanie glanced at Jane. "I was planning on inviting her to sit with us at lunch on her first day, but she never showed up in the cafeteria."

That was just like Stephanie – she was
a great organizer and loved helping people.

"Jane looks so lonely sitting there by herself,"
Emma said. "She must be terribly bored.
Even her clothes look boring! I wish I could
help her."

Andrea grinned. "Uh oh – are you planning
another makeover?"

"Maybe even a social makeover?"
Stephanie added with a laugh.

Emma laughed, too. She loved doing
makeovers on herself, her friends, her
pets, or just about anyone else. Usually they
turned out well, though occasionally things
went wrong – like the time she'd weaved
colourful spring flowers into Olivia's brown
hair, which looked amazing but attracted all
kinds of buzzing insects.

"Not a makeover, exactly," Emma said. "I just want to make sure Jane's shyness doesn't stop her from having fun on this trip."

"That's really sweet, Emma," Olivia said. "I think we should do it!"

"Me, too," Stephanie agreed. "And you're the perfect person to lead the way, Emma. You're

so sweet and sensitive and fun to be around
that you're sure to bring Jane out of her shell."

"Thanks, guys." Emma blushed, happy that
her friends were saying such nice things.
"I guess all I can do is try. It'll be fun!"

2
Welcome
to the Sunshine Ranch

"I think we're here!" Emma said as the bus slowed down, turned off the highway and trundled down a bumpy road. They passed fields with cows grazing, and then they saw a market stall overloaded with fruit and vegetables.

Stephanie let out a loud cheer. "We're here!" she cried, pumping her fist.

All around the bus, other

students joined in, whooping and clapping. Emma shivered with excitement. She couldn't wait to see the ranch!

The bus headed up a long, winding driveway and under a rustic wooden sign that read, 'SUNSHINE RANCH: Welcome friends!' with little suns carved at either end.

Emma noticed that Jane was the only person who wasn't crowding towards the windows to get a look. She was just sitting there, looking at her hands. That made Emma more determined than ever to help the new girl fit in. Nobody should be lonely on a fun class trip!

The bus pulled to a stop in front of a big red barn with an arched doorway – above that was a smaller door that stood open, revealing stacks of fluffy golden hay in the loft. Tidy rows of pretty fruit trees stood to one side of the barn and on the other, sleek horses were eating hay in a white-fenced corral.

"Wow, those horses are so beautiful!" Mia exclaimed.

Andrea giggled. "You think all horses are beautiful," she said.

Mia laughed, too. "Well, they are!"

Ms Palmer, the school headteacher, stood and clapped her hands for attention. "All right, everyone," she said, "we have a lot of interesting activities planned for you today.

First, I want everyone to choose a buddy. After you've paired off, you can head into the barn and wait there."

"Uh oh." Olivia sounded worried. "There are five of us – one of us won't be able to buddy up."

"Don't worry," Emma said.

27

"I'll ask Jane to be my buddy."

Stephanie's eyes lit up. "Perfect!"

Emma jumped out of her seat to find Jane. Jane was still staring at her hands when Emma jumped in front of her.

"Hi," Emma said brightly. "I'm Emma. Do you want to be my buddy?"

Jane looked up at her in surprise. "Oh!" she said. "Um, sure. I guess."

"Great!" Emma grabbed her hand. "Come on, let's go and check out the barn — it looks really cool!"

She dragged Jane off the bus and through the big doorway. The barn seemed even more enormous inside, with a huge open space in the middle, horses in stalls on the right and more doors on the left. Several of Emma's classmates were already in the barn too, looking at the horses or examining a map

of the ranch that was hanging on the wall.
A friendly cat had also wandered out to greet
the visitors.

"Wow," Emma said. "This place is cool!"

She glanced at Jane, but the new girl didn't
answer. She just nodded,
then looked down
at her feet.

Uh oh, Emma thought.
She really is shy!

Just then her friends
joined them. "Andrea
and I are buddies," Mia
announced.

"Right. That means Olivia was stuck with
me," Stephanie joked, nudging Olivia in
the side.

Emma smiled, but then she noticed that
Jane looked confused. "These are my friends,"

Emma told the new girl. "Stephanie is the one in the cute striped shirt, Mia's the redhead with the green tank and tan capris, Olivia is wearing the pink and white shirt, and that's Andrea in the turquoise top and jeans."

"And Emma is the one who's totally obsessed with fashion, in case you couldn't guess," Mia told Jane with a grin.

Emma blushed, realizing she'd just described her friends by what they were wearing.

"I'm not *totally* obsessed with fashion," she objected. Then she smiled. "Just a *little* obsessed."

Suddenly, the headteacher, Ms Palmer whistled loudly to get everyone's attention. "Do you all have buddies?" she called. "Good. Feel free to look around the barn for a few minutes. The ranch manager will be with us soon to start the day's activities."

"I wonder what we'll do first," Stephanie said as the friends wandered further into the barn. A cute dapple-grey pony stuck her head out over one of the stall doors, and Emma stepped over to give her a pat.

"I hope we can ride that one," Mia replied eagerly. "I can't wait to learn Western."

Emma smiled at her buddy. "Do you like horses, Jane?"

"I guess so." Jane glanced at the toilet sign nearby. "Um, excuse me for a minute, OK? I need to go to the bathroom." Without waiting for a response, Jane scurried away and disappeared into the girls' toilet.

Mia raised one eyebrow. "She seems really shy."

The others agreed. Emma felt worried.

"Guys, Jane might be more challenging than I thought," she said. "What if I can't do it? What if I can't work out how to bring her out of her shell?"

"You can do it," Stephanie told

her. "Especially with all of us behind you."

Emma felt a little better. "OK, then hurry – give me some ideas before she gets back. What should I do?"

Olivia looked thoughtful. "I think you need a plan," she said. "She's a pretty tough case, so you'll

probably need to be organized about it."

Stephanie waved one hand, as if shooing away Olivia's idea. "I like being organized as much as anybody, but this is absent-minded Emma we're talking about, remember?" she said with a laugh. "All you have to do is ask her lots of questions, Emma. Everyone likes to talk about themselves, right? So get her talking, and pretty soon she'll forget about being shy."

"Hmm." Emma had to admit that sounded like a pretty good plan. "I guess I could try that. Anyone else?"

Andrea shrugged. "I think Steph might be right. Everyone likes being the centre of attention. Just look for ways to make Jane feel that way, and you should—"

Mia cleared her throat loudly. Jane was walking back over.

Emma waved at her, smiling brightly. "We're over here, Jane!" she called.

Nearby, Chelsea Noble was sitting on a bench with a couple of her snooty friends. She wrinkled her nose. "Settle down, Emma," Chelsea said loudly. "Just because you're in a barn right now, doesn't mean you have to act like you were born in one."

Her friends started laughing loudly. Emma just rolled her eyes.

"Don't let Chelsea's nasty comments bother you, Emma," Olivia said quietly.

"Don't worry, I never do," said Emma. Just then, she spotted a tall man in a cowboy hat strolling into the barn.

Mia saw him, too. "That's Grandma and Grandpa's ranch manager, I think," she said.

"Great!" Emma said. "I can't wait to hear what we're going to do first!"

"And what about your Grandparents, Mia? Are they at the ranch?" Stephanie asked. "I would love to meet them."

"Me, too," Andrea added. "And me, and me. . . " the other girls joined.

"Unfortunately, not this time," Mia said. "They've gone to the Farmer Fairs and will be back in two days or so. But don't worry. We can come and visit them any time you want."

The girls cheered, clapping their hands. "We'll hold you to that!"

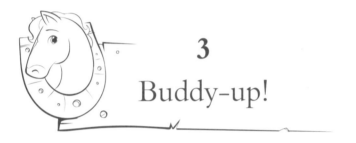

3
Buddy-up!

The ranch manager was tanned and dressed in faded blue jeans, a checked shirt and a cowboy hat. Emma noticed right away that he was wearing real cowboy boots too. They were brown leather with a pointy toe and curly patterns on the sides – and they were pretty dusty! Big silver spurs on the heels clanked and jingled as he walked.

The manager stood in front of the students and his face broke into a big smile that made the corners of his eyes crinkle. "Welcome to the Sunshine Ranch, kids," he said, tipping

his cowboy hat at the group. "My name's Jack
Stockwell, but you can call me Cowboy Jack.
We're all real glad you could come spend the
day with us. Now, are you ready
to have some fun?"

"Yeah!" Emma cheered
along with the others.

Well, most of the
others. Emma looked
over at Jane, but she was just
standing there with her
arms crossed.

"Good," Cowboy Jack
said. "Now, you're a pretty
big group, so we're going to
split you up for the different
activities. But don't worry,
you'll all get a chance to try
everything over the course of

the day. Then we'll get together again for the big barn dance this evening, where you'll do some square dancing."

"Square dancing?" Andrea's green eyes lit up with interest. "Cool!"

Cowboy Jack pointed to a big wooden barrel. "Let's have one member of each buddy team come up here and pick a ticket out of the barrel. That'll tell you which activity your team will be trying first. Got it?"

"Got it!" called out a boy named Jacob, the class joker. "I hope I get to try riding a bucking bronco!"

That made everyone laugh, including Cowboy Jack. "All right, young man," the manager said. "Why don't you come up and choose your ticket first?"

Jacob hurried forward. "That's Jacob," Emma told Jane. "He's kind of goofy sometimes, but

he's really nice. He takes flying lessons with
Stephanie at the flight school."

"Oh," Jane said.

Emma waited for her to ask questions
about Jacob or the flying lessons. Or make
a comment about Cowboy Jack and the day's
activities. Or say anything else at all. But the
new girl remained silent.

Meanwhile, Jacob fished a slip of paper out
of the barrel. "Cool – we're going riding!"
he said after he checked the paper.

"Awesome!" yelled his buddy. "Hey Jacob, maybe if you're lucky your horse will turn out to be a bucking bronco!"

After that, more people stepped forward to choose their activities. "Come on, let's get in the queue," Stephanie said eagerly. "I'll pick for us, OK Olivia?"

"Sure, go for it," Olivia agreed.

"Go ahead," Mia told Andrea. "You can pick for our team."

Emma glanced at Jane. "Do you want to pick for us?"

"No, that's OK," Jane said quietly. "You can do it."

Emma shrugged. "OK."

She stepped forward with Stephanie and Andrea. Each of them reached into the barrel and pulled out a slip of paper. As soon as Stephanie glanced at hers, she smiled.

"Ooh, we're going apple picking first," she said. "What did you guys get?"

"Looks like Mia and I will be doing some Western riding with Jacob," Andrea said. "Emma? How about you?"

Emma read her piece of paper. "Campfire songs."

"Too bad we're not together." Andrea looked a little disappointed. "I wish we could all do the same thing at the same time."

"Me too," Emma agreed, sneaking a peek at Jane. She would have liked to have her friends around to help her cheer up Jane.

Stephanie leaned closer. "Don't worry," she whispered. "You'll do fine with Jane. Just remember to ask her lots of questions about herself. That should break the ice."

"How'd you guess what I was thinking?" Emma asked with a laugh.

Stephanie winked. "I must be psychic."

"Nope," Andrea put in. "Just a good friend."

The three of them returned to their buddies. Mia was chattering away about the horses she'd seen in the corral. Olivia was nodding and asking questions, but Jane was just standing there listening.

"Come on, Jane." Emma took her buddy by the arm. "We got campfire songs. Let's go and find the campfire."

She grabbed Jane by the hand and headed towards the map on the back wall.

44

Emma scanned it carefully. There were
lots of different locations marked on it. For
a moment, Emma's gaze lingered on something
called the Cowboy Costume Corral. She loved
dressing up!

"Look," she said, spotting what she was
looking for. "I see something called Campfire
Corner. That must be where we – hey!" She
stopped short as someone pushed past her.

It was Chelsea. "Where's the henhouse?" she
demanded. "We're supposed to be collecting
eggs, but we don't know where
to go. They really ought to be
more organized around here."

"Come on, Jane." Emma
frowned at Chelsea, then
grabbed her partner's hand
again. "Let's go and check out
Campfire Corner."

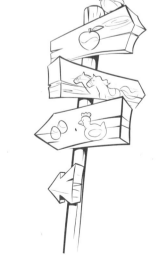

Emma led the way out of the barn. There were signs pointing off in every direction, including one that read CAMPFIRE CORNER: THAT WAY.

It didn't take long to find. It was a clearing amongst some pine trees, with a big fire pit in the middle and logs arranged in a circle for people to sit on. Several sets of buddies were already seated, chattering excitedly and pointing at the fire burning in the pit. A young blonde woman with a ponytail was tossing more wood on to the fire. She looked up as Emma and Jane found seats on an empty log.

"Welcome!" the woman called. "Make yourselves comfortable. We'll get started as soon as the guitarist arrives."

"OK, thanks," Emma said. She was kind of glad that the activity wasn't going to

start right away. That gave her a chance to put Stephanie's advice into action. "So Jane," she said, turning to her buddy. "Where did you live before you moved to Heartlake City?"

Jane looked a little surprised at the question. "Fort Harbourview," she said. "Why?"

"Just wondering," Emma said brightly. "How long did you live there?"

"My whole life." Jane sounded a little sad now. Uh oh – Emma didn't want to make her miss her old home town. She wanted to help her fit in in her new one!

"Um…" She searched her mind for a happier question. "Do you have any pets?"

"I have a fishtank," Jane said. "I'm not allowed to have any other pets."

"Really?" Emma laughed. "Don't let Mia hear that! She loves animals. I mean, I love animals, too – who doesn't, right? But Mia loves them even more than most people. She wants to be a veterinarian when she grows up, or maybe a zookeeper, or a dog trainer. Or a professional horse rider – she's really good at riding. She even has her own horse named Bella, and they always win lots of ribbons at the shows, and –"

"Attention, please!" The blonde woman clapped her hands. Cowboy Jack was standing next to her holding a red guitar. "We're ready to get started."

Emma realized she'd barely let Jane answer any questions

before she started chattering about herself and her friends. Oops! She sneaked a look at the shy girl, who was watching as the guitarist plucked a few strings to tune up. Emma swallowed a sigh. She was going to have to do a lot better if she wanted to help Jane feel comfortable in her new home.

4
Campfire Songs

For a little while, Emma forgot all about her project. The campfire songs activity was a lot of fun. The blonde woman and the guitarist spent the first few minutes talking about how cowboys liked to entertain themselves on long cattle drives by singing songs around the campfire. Then the pair taught the group lots of old cowboy songs like 'Ballad of Dallas', 'The Wild Horse', and 'Cowboy's Trails'.

Emma was having lots of fun singing along at the top of her voice. Jane on the other hand didn't sing very loudly, although Emma could see her tapping her foot and swaying along with the music. Good, Emma thought with a secret smile. That means she likes music. Maybe I can ask her questions about that later.

"OK, we're running out of time," Cowboy Jack said, checking his watch. "But I think we can squeeze in one more song. It's one of my favourites – 'Home on the Ranch.'"

"Ooh, I know that one!" a girl called out. "We sang it all the time at summer camp."

"Great!" the blonde woman said. "You can help us teach it to the others, OK? Then anyone who wants to try a solo can take a turn singing the chorus."

"OK." The girl smiled and stood up. "I'm not sure I remember all the words, though."

As she listened to the girl sing, Emma leaned closer to Jane. "Andrea will love this activity," she whispered. "She's a great singer. And she loves doing solos!"

Thinking about Andrea reminded Emma of something. Andrea had said that everyone loved being the centre of attention, and that Emma should look for ways to make Jane feel that way. Maybe this campfire song was a way to do that!

When the guitarist asked who wanted to try a solo, a boy from Emma's history class quickly volunteered. While he was singing the song's chorus, Emma nudged Jane.

"You should volunteer next," she whispered.

"What? No!" Jane exclaimed softly.

"Oh, come on – it'll be fun!" Emma said. As soon as the boy had finished his turn at the solo, she raised her hand. "My partner wants to try," she called out.

"No I don't," Jane said quickly. "Really."

Cowboy Jack smiled at the two girls.

"Why don't you two do a duet, then?" he said. "You can sing together."

"Sure, that sounds like fun," Emma said. "We'll do it. Right, Jane?"

Jane looked nervous. But finally she nodded.

"OK," she said softly. "I guess that'll be fine."

"Good." The guitarist strummed a chord. "I'll get you started…" He began singing the first verse, along with the blonde woman and the rest of the group. When it was almost time for the chorus, Emma reached over and squeezed Jane's hand.

"Ready?" Emma whispered.

Jane didn't say anything, but she nodded.

A second later it was their turn. Emma cleared her throat and sang the first few lines of the chorus.

Beside her, Emma could hear Jane singing softly. Her voice wasn't nearly as rich and full as Andrea's, or even as loud and confident as Emma's own voice. But it was sweet and melodic. Emma hoped everybody else could hear, but she was afraid they couldn't. Jane was singing too quietly to be the centre of attention.

Suddenly, Emma had another idea. When they reached the final line of the chorus, Emma stopped singing. Jane's voice rang out alone in the silence.

"And the sun is shining all day!"

Jane gasped when she realized she was singing solo. She clapped her hands over her mouth, her blue eyes wide with horror.

"That was great!" Emma exclaimed, patting her on the back. "I knew you'd sound amazing."

She started clapping, and most of the other people around the campfire did the same. Emma expected Jane to smile, maybe even take a bow like Andrea did after all her performances.

But instead, Jane's eyes filled with tears. "I – I can't believe you did that," she cried out. "I'm so embarrassed!"

"What? But why?" Emma's smile faded.
"You sounded terrific!"

Jane didn't say another word. With a loud
sob, she jumped off the log and ran out of
the circle.

♥ ♥ ♥

It took Emma a while to find Jane. The new girl was huddled behind a rosebush, sniffling and dabbing at her eyes with a tissue.

"I'm so sorry," Emma exclaimed. "But I don't get it. Why'd you get so upset?"

"I don't like singing in front of people," Jane said, glaring at her. "But you forced me to do it anyway! That's not nice. Were you trying to make me look stupid in front of everyone?"

"What? No, of course not!" Emma bit her lip, feeling terrible. She realized she'd made a big mistake. Jane was so shy – no wonder she didn't like being the centre of attention! "I'm so sorry, Jane. Really, I am. I promise I didn't mean to make you feel bad. Will you forgive me? Pretty please?"

Jane looked cross for another moment. Then her expression softened.

"OK, I guess," she said. "Sorry I thought you were trying to be mean."

"It's OK." Emma grabbed her hand and

squeezed it. "And thanks. Now come on – we're supposed to go and pick our next activity out of the barrel."

5

Friendly Advice

Emma and Jane hurried into the barn. Most of their classmates were already there. Some were over by the barrel picking their next activities. Others were gathered around the map trying to figure out where to go.

Emma spotted her friends over near the map and waved. "Let's go and see how the other activities were," she said, pulling Jane over.

"Hi," Stephanie said when the pair reached the group. "Did you two have fun singing around the campfire?"

"Um, yeah." Emma shot a look at Jane, not

wanting to go into detail. She'd have to tell her friends about her big mistake later, when it wouldn't embarrass Jane even more. "How were your activities?"

"Great!" Mia exclaimed. "Western riding is really fun. We learned how to put on the Western saddle, and how to neck rein, and we even got to try some roping."

"Yeah, and now I wish we had Western shows at Heartlake Stables," Andrea added. "The outfits they wear are really cool. Some of the shirts are almost as sparkly as my stage costumes!"

"Stage costumes?" Jane spoke up, looking interested. "Are you a dancer or something?"

Emma laughed. "Andrea's a born performer – she does a little of everything," she explained. "Like I was telling you before, she's especially good at singing." She turned to Olivia and Stephanie. "How was apple picking?"

"Fun," Stephanie said. "I can't believe how many different kinds of apples they grow here!"

Olivia nodded. "We got to taste most of the different kinds, too," she added with a grin.

"Awesome." Emma glanced towards the barrel. "So when do we pick our next activities?"

"We already picked ours." Stephanie held up a slip of paper. "Olivia and I are doing a nature hike."

"And we're collecting eggs from the henhouse and learning about all the other animals on the ranch," Andrea said. "Other than the horses, of course — we already did that."

"Sounds great." Emma glanced at Jane. "Why don't you pick for us this time, since I did it last time."

"OK." Jane hurried off across the barn and Emma waited until she was out of earshot before turning to her friends.

"Listen, guys," she said, leaning forward so nobody else would overhear. "I'm still having trouble getting Jane to relax and have fun."

"Really?" Stephanie looked surprised.

Emma nodded and sighed. "I'm trying to take Steph's advice and ask her lots of questions," she said. "But there wasn't a lot of time for talking during our first activity. So do you have any other ideas?"

"Maybe you'll be lucky and get an animal activity, like us," Mia said. "It's easy to bond over taking care of animals."

"True," Olivia agreed. "That's kind of how I became friends with you guys, remember?"

Emma smiled. She did remember. Olivia had been chasing after her lively puppy when the other girls had first met her. "That's a great idea," Emma said. "Everyone loves animals, and Jane already told me she has pet fish. Anyone else have any tips?"

"I still think it might help to be organized," Olivia said. "I always feel more comfortable when I have a real plan before I do something. Maybe Jane is like that, too."

"Hmm. You could be right," Emma said. Olivia was super-logical and loved science. Emma wasn't like that at all – she was an artist at heart, and loved to be spontaneous and figure things out as she went along, whether she was putting together an outfit or painting a sunset. But what if Jane was more like Olivia? That would explain why she hadn't liked her surprise campfire solo. Maybe it wasn't just because she was shy – maybe it was because she liked to be prepared and logical about things, just like Olivia.

Just then, she saw Jane walking back over. "What did you get?" Andrea asked the new girl.

Jane showed them the piece of paper. "Horseback riding," she said. "I just hope I can do it."

"Of course you can!" Emma grabbed her hand. "You can do anything you put your mind to. Have you ever ridden before?"

"No," Jane said. "My parents didn't think it was a good idea to spend much time in a barn, because I —"

"What?" Mia interrupted with mock dismay. "That's terrible! You'd better get over to the corral right away so you can catch up with the rest of us!" Emma giggled. "She's right. Let's go!"

A small crowd was gathered near the horse corral waiting for the riding activity to start. Emma waved to a few friends, then pulled Jane closer to the corral.

"I probably shouldn't get so close," Jane said, eyeing the horses with a nervous smile.

"It's OK," Emma said. "I know horses are big, but most of them are really sweet." She reached over the fence to pat a gleaming chestnut foal. "See? He just wants to be friends."

"It's not that," Jane said. "I just don't think I —"

"Attention, everyone!" Cowboy Jack called out, striding into view. "Ready to get started?" He grinned as Emma and most of the others cheered. "Good. Now, has anyone here ever ridden a horse before?"

Emma raised her hand. She didn't ride as often as Mia or Stephanie, but she enjoyed taking a lesson or going on a nice trail ride at Heartlake Stables now and again. Several of her

classmates also stuck their hands in the air or
yelled, "Me!"

"Good, good," Cowboy Jack said. "Now, has
anyone here ever ridden Western before?"

This time only one boy raised his hand.
He explained that his family had once gone on
a two-week holiday to a dude ranch! Everyone
oohed and ahhed at that.

Cowboy Jack went on to explain some of
the basic differences between Western and
English riding. Emma listened with interest,
but kept part of her attention on Jane.
The new girl had sidled away from the fence
during Cowboy Jack's
talk. Now she was as far
from the horses as she
could get.

Emma bit her lip. Jane seemed really scared. How could the two of them bond over animals, as Mia had suggested, if Jane wouldn't even get near a horse?

When Cowboy Jack finished his talk, he instructed each buddy pair to select a horse. They could start brushing their horse while he went around and showed each pair how to put on the big Western saddle.

"Cool," Emma said, rushing into the corral. "Let's take the cute little bay mare over there."

Jane hung back by the gate. "Listen, Emma," she said. "I just don't think I can do this."

"Don't be silly!" Emma grabbed her arm and dragged her over to the mare. "Here, give her a pat."

Jane let out a shriek, yanking her hand back. "Stop!" she yelled, her face going red. "I said I can't do this."

Emma blinked, startled by the other girl's reaction. "But…"

Cowboy Jack had heard the scream. He hurried over, a worried look on his face. "Is everything all right over here?"

"Sure, we're fine," Emma began. "I'm just trying to show Jane that –"

"Everything's not all right," Jane interrupted, glaring at Emma. "I keep trying to tell her, but she won't listen. I'm really allergic to horses!"

6

Super Organized

The rest of the Western riding activity was fun, but Emma didn't enjoy it quite as much as she normally would have. She was distracted by what had happened with Jane. The whole thing made her feel terrible. Jane had been trying to tell her all along that she couldn't go near the horses, but Emma hadn't stopped talking long enough to listen. She would have to do better from now on, or she'd never be able to help Jane fit in!

After hearing about Jane's allergy, Cowboy Jack had suggested she sit and watch the

others from a safe distance. As Emma brushed
the bay mare after her ride, she could see
the new girl perched on a bench between
the corral and the parking lot. She looked
small and lonely sitting there by
herself, which only made
Emma more determined to
help her.

She just wasn't sure
how. Usually her best
friends were great at
figuring out how to do
just about anything.
But so far, their
advice wasn't
working.
Andrea's
idea had
totally

backfired, since Jane didn't seem to like being the centre of attention. And Mia's plan to bond over animals wouldn't work either now that Emma knew Jane couldn't go near anything with fur or feathers without breaking out in a rash!

As soon as Cowboy Jack dismissed the group, Emma hurried over to the bench. "Listen, Jane," she said. "I have to apologize again. I never would have tried to make you touch that horse if I knew you were allergic to animals."

"It's OK." Jane offered her a small smile. "My parents are always saying I need to speak up for myself more. I should have made you listen before things went that far."

Emma was relieved that Jane didn't seem angry. "Well, I'll try to listen more from now on," she said, returning the smile. "Want to go in and pick our next activity?"

"Sure." Jane stood up and followed Emma into the barn.

Emma's friends were there too, talking about their latest adventures. They all looked surprised when they heard about Jane's allergy. Emma noticed all of her friends giving her questioning looks, but there was no chance to talk privately. That also meant Emma couldn't ask them for more advice.

Instead, she thought over what they'd already told her. She could try Stephanie's advice again. Maybe if she'd asked Jane more questions earlier, she would have known about that allergy!

Then she remembered Olivia's advice to be organized and logical. Maybe it was time to give that a try.

"It's your turn to pick our next activity," Jane said, interrupting Emma's thoughts.

"Oh! OK." Emma hurried over to the barrel and selected a slip of paper. She rejoined the others, then unfolded it.

"What's it say?" Andrea asked.

"Apple picking." Emma held it up so they could all see.

Stephanie clapped her hands. "Oh, you'll have fun doing that," she said.

"Yeah," Olivia agreed, smiling at Jane. "And there are no animals in that one."

"That's good." Jane smiled back, then turned to Emma. "Should we head over to the orchard?"

"Sure, let's go." As Emma followed her partner out of the barn, she was still thinking about Olivia's advice. She wished she'd had a chance to talk to her about it. How would Emma act if she were logical and scientific like Olivia?

When they reached the gate leading into the orchard, a cheerful-looking older woman was standing there. She had greyish-brown hair

and was wearing a gingham dress with an apron over it.

"Ah!" the woman said when Emma and Jane joined the group of students gathered near the gate, including Chelsea and her partner. "It looks like our last pair is here."

"Sorry we're late," Emma said, glancing around at the others.

"No problem," Chelsea said, rolling her eyes. "We all just love waiting around for you."

The woman ignored Chelsea's sarcastic comment. "I'm Mrs Marks," she said to the group. "I'll be showing you around our orchard and letting you taste some of our delicious apple varieties."

She led them into the orchard, stopping near a table with posters about apples set up on it. The table also held lots of plates containing apple slices and a big pile of mesh bags. Mrs Marks talked all about apples and the other types of fruit grown on the ranch. But Emma was only half listening. She was still trying to figure out how to follow Olivia's advice.

Suddenly a gasp went up from the whole group. Emma blinked, realizing she must have missed something.

"What happened?" she asked Jane.

But as she turned to look at her partner, she was surprised to find Jane was no longer standing next to her. Instead, she was several feet away – holding a bright red apple in her hand!

"Didn't you see? It was totally awesome!" said a boy next to Jane. "That apple was falling from the tree, and she jumped over and caught it before it hit Chelsea in the head!"

"Yes, that was quite impressive," Mrs Marks said with a chuckle. "You're very graceful, young lady!"

"Thanks." Jane blushed and handed the apple to the woman.

Uh oh. Emma gulped. Jane was becoming the centre of attention again. Emma had to put a stop to that before the shy girl got too self-conscious. "Excuse me!" she called out loudly.

"What kind of apple is that, Mrs Marks?"

Chelsea gave Emma a strange look. "Who cares?' she said. "It's the apple that almost gave me concussion."

"Yeah, you owe her one, Chelsea," Matthew said with a grin. "She saved your life! Or at least saved you from a headache."

"Oh. Right." Chelsea frowned slightly, then glanced at Jane. "Thanks."

"You're welcome," Jane said softly.

"All right, then, let's move on…" Mrs Marks finished up her talk by explaining that the kids were going to spend the rest of the hour learning more about the apple orchard. "You can wander around and pick whichever apples you like," she said. Then she smiled and waggled a finger playfully. "But only a dozen apples per pair, please! So choose carefully."

That gave Emma an idea. "OK," she said to Jane as Mrs Marks starting handing out mesh bags. "We should plan out our strategy."

"Our strategy?" Jane looked confused as she slung a bag over her shoulder. "What do you mean?"

"I mean we need to be logical about this." Emma could almost hear Olivia in her head. "We need a plan. Otherwise we might not get all the best kinds of apples."

"Oh." Jane shrugged. "I figured we'd just wander around and pick whichever apples look good. When we have a dozen, we'll stop."

"We could do that," Emma agreed, glancing around at the pretty little apple trees with their shiny red fruit.

For a second, she was
tempted to go along
with Jane's suggestion.
It sounded like fun to wander
through the orchard choosing the nicest
looking apples. But then she remembered:
she was supposed to be logical and Olivia-like.

"No, but it's better to have a plan and follow
it," she said firmly. "I think we should taste all
the different kinds of apples first. Then we can
walk around the orchard and figure out where
each kind is growing. That way we'll be sure to
get all our favourites."

Jane still looked dubious, but she shrugged.
"OK, I guess that'll work."

While the other kids scattered among the
trees, Emma and Jane headed over to the table.
Mrs Marks looked surprised to see them.
"Hungry already, girls?" she asked.

Emma nodded. "We'd like to taste all the apples, please," she announced. "If that's OK? We thought it would help us decide which kinds to pick."

"Of course." Mrs Marks waved a hand at the plates on the table. "Help yourselves."

"Thanks." Emma stepped forward,

reaching for a tasty-looking apple slice. Then she stopped. "We should be organized about this, too," she said aloud.

"Huh?" Jane glanced at her. She was already chewing a bite of apple.

"We should start at one end of the table and work our way over," Emma said. "We might even want to take notes."

"Notes?" Jane sounded dubious. "Um, OK."

Emma dug into her purse for a piece of paper. "All right," she said briskly, feeling very logical and scientific. Olivia would be so proud of her! "The first type is Gala. Let's both taste it and then write down what we think…"

7

Yee-haw!

"How was apple picking?" Stephanie asked as Emma and Jane rejoined the others in the barn an hour later. "Wasn't it great?"

Emma shrugged. Apple picking hadn't been quite as much fun as she'd been expecting. It was exhausting trying to keep track of all those varieties and search out the exact ones they wanted. Worst of all, Jane hadn't seemed to enjoy it much, either. She'd barely said a word the whole time.

"It was OK," Emma told her friends. "I'm looking forward to trying something else, though."

Olivia held up a slip of paper. "Both our teams got the roping show this time," she said, sounding excited. "Maybe you guys will get it, too!"

"I hope so," Emma said. She really meant it, too. For one thing, she always had more fun when she was with all her friends. And for another, they might be able to help her figure out how to help Jane.

"I'll go and pick for us," Jane offered, hurrying away towards the barrel.

Mia watched her go. "So how's it going?" she asked Emma quietly.

"Not so well." Emma sighed. "Every time I think she's finally starting to have fun, something else happens to wreck things." She grimaced. "For instance, Chelsea's head got in the way of an apple, and it ended up with everyone staring at Jane…"

She told her friends the story. "Wow," Andrea said with a giggle. "Too bad Jane doesn't know Chelsea that well. Otherwise she would've just let that apple hit her!"

"Very funny." Stephanie grinned at Andrea. "Not very nice, but very funny."

Emma glanced at Olivia. "And I tried your idea to make a logical plan and stick to it, but I don't think it worked. Jane didn't seem to have much fun."

"Oops," Olivia said. "Maybe she's more of a free spirit like you, Emma."

Stephanie squeezed Emma's arm. "It was worth a try, though."

Mia cleared her throat loudly. "Here comes Jane. And she doesn't look too happy."

"Our slip says 'Chickens and Eggs,'" Jane announced when she reached the group.

"Oh, we did that," Andrea said. "It was fun."

Mia nodded. "You learn a lot about chickens. You even get to hold one if you want, and pick up fresh eggs from the henhouse. Plus you'll see some goats and pigs, and watch the ranch dog herd some sheep."

Jane bit her lip. "I don't think I can do any of that," she said. "My allergies…"

"Oh! Right." For a second, Emma felt relieved. If Jane had to sit out this activity like she had the riding one, that meant Emma could focus on having fun for a while instead of trying to entertain the new girl.

But she immediately felt guilty. It was pretty clear that Jane wasn't having a good time on this trip so far, and at least part of that was Emma's fault. She had to figure out a way to turn things around.

95

But how? Nothing her friends suggested seemed to work. She stared at the map of the ranch, and suddenly an idea popped into her head. Maybe it was time to come up with a plan of her own...

"I know," she blurted out. "Let's ask Cowboy Jack if we can skip the chicken activity and look around the ranch instead. I saw something called the Cowboy Costume Corral on the map – that could be fun to check out."

Mia looked surprised. "Are you sure you want to do that? I bet they'd let you choose a new slip out of the barrel, since Jane has allergies."

"Yeah," Stephanie added. "You haven't done the nature walk yet, right?"

"Or you might end up watching the roping demonstration with us," Olivia added.

For a second Emma hesitated, but then she shook her head. She'd tried her friends' ideas;

now she wanted to give her own plan a shot.

"No, this will be fun." She grabbed Jane's hand. "Come on, let's go ask. See you guys later!"

Cowboy Jack was talking to their headteacher Palmer over near the main doors. When they heard Emma's request, the headteacher looked dubious.

"I don't know," she said. "We can't have students just wandering around by themselves…"

But Cowboy Jack was rubbing his chin thoughtfully. "I didn't realize one of our guests had such severe allergies," he said. "We really don't have enough activities for her without the animal ones. Maybe the Cowboy Costume Corral isn't such a bad idea. We didn't put it on the schedule because there's not enough room for a big group in there, but there's no reason these two couldn't spend the next hour there."

"Hmm. What is this Costume Corral?" the headteacher asked.

"It's where visitors can dress up in authentic Western outfits and have their pictures taken," Cowboy Jack explained. "A lot of people seem to enjoy it."

Ms Palmer smiled at Emma. "I see. Well, I have a feeling Emma will definitely enjoy something like that. If it's all right with you, it's all right with me."

"Yay!" Emma cheered. "Thanks, Ms P!"

Soon Cowboy Jack was letting Emma and Jane into the Cowboy Costume Corral. It was a small outbuilding near the campfire area. All four walls were packed with racks, trunks, and shelves full of clothes. In the centre of the room was a full-length mirror and an old-fashioned camera on a tripod.

"I'm afraid we don't have anyone to help

you, or to work the camera," Cowboy Jack said. "Are you sure you'll be OK by yourselves?"

"We'll be fine," Emma assured him. "Thanks!"

As soon as the manager hurried out, Emma started looking around. This was going to be fun. There was nothing she liked better than a good makeover, and this was the perfect place for one – cowgirl style!

"Check it out," she said. "There's cool stage makeup and everything!"

"Stage make-up?" Jane didn't sound very enthusiastic. "That stuff always looks so fake

unless you're actually on stage."

"Don't worry, it'll be fun." Emma grabbed
a tube of lip gloss and uncapped it. "Ooh, this
colour would look great on you!"

For the next twenty minutes, Emma worked hard turning Jane into a cute cowgirl. She found her a black-and-white pony-print fringed vest to slip on over her white T-shirt, and a pair of matching chaps that strapped over her jeans. Next she added a white leather belt studded with sparkly pink rhinestones. Then Emma selected a pair of pink tooled cowgirl boots from the racks along one wall and insisted Jane kick off her sneakers and put them on. A pink felt cowgirl hat completed the look.

After that, Emma returned to the make up area. She dusted glittery powder over Jane's whole face, then added a sheen of candy-pink gloss to her lips and just a touch of rosy blush to her cheeks.

"Perfect!" she declared at last, stepping back for a better look. "You're ready to pose for the cover of Cute Cowgirl magazine!"

"Is that really a thing?" Jane asked.

Emma laughed. "I don't know. But it should be! Anyway, go ahead – strike a pose."

"Are you kidding? I feel silly enough already," Jane said. But she was smiling a little beneath her broad-brimmed hat.

"Go for it," Emma urged. "You know you want to!"

Jane laughed. She did a little spin and then leaped up, clicking the heels of her cowgirl boots together. "Yee-haw!" she exclaimed, rolling her eyes.

"What's going on in here?" a new voice said.

Emma froze. She knew that voice. "Chelsea?" she said, spinning around. "What are you doing here?"

"I was trying to find my way to the bathroom." Chelsea leaned against the doorframe and smirked. "But I heard noise in here and decided to see what was going on."

Emma shot a look at Jane, who had yanked off her hat and was staring at the ground. The new girl's cheeks were bright pink, and it had nothing to do with the blush Emma had just applied to them.

Emma gritted her teeth. Why did Chelsea have to walk in right now – just as Jane was finally starting to have fun?

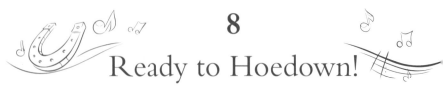

8
Ready to Hoedown!

"Where's Jane?" Mia asked, setting her tray of food down beside Emma's. Andrea, Olivia, and Stephanie were already seated at the long wooden table.

Emma grimaced. "Good question. I think she's avoiding me."

It was dinnertime. The entire class had gathered in the dining hall, a large, rustic building on the far side of the parking lot. As soon as Emma and Jane had entered, Jane had muttered something about going to look for a napkin and never came back.

Emma wasn't surprised. Even though Chelsea had left the Cowboy Costume Corral without doing much more than smirking, things hadn't been the same after that. Jane had taken off her cowgirl clothes and then gone to the bathroom to wash off her make up. That had taken her a long time – so long that by the time she returned, it was time to head back to the barn to choose their next activity.

Things hadn't gone much better for the rest of the afternoon. Their next activity had been a nature walk. Jane had stayed close to the guide,

106

which meant Emma didn't have a chance to talk to her. Then they'd gone to the roping demonstration. Emma had found seats in the front row, but soon after the show started, Jane had moved back a few rows, claiming she needed to be farther away from the horses. Emma had offered to go with her, but Jane had insisted she'd be fine by herself.

"I wish I could have figured out how to help her," Emma said with a sigh. "But it looks like I'll have to admit it – Jane is going to be my first totally failed makeover."

"Don't beat yourself up," Olivia told Emma with sympathy in her brown eyes. "You tried everything you could."

"But it wasn't enough." Emma stirred her chilli. It was delicious, but she wasn't feeling very hungry. "I didn't help her make any friends. Or even have much fun."

Andrea glanced around the dining hall. "I don't know how anyone could help having fun at a place like this. I loved everything we did today – especially the campfire songs."

"That was fun," Olivia agreed. "But I liked the nature walk the best."

"Are you kidding?" Mia looked up from her food. "The Western riding was definitely the coolest activity we did all day!"

Stephanie laughed. "You're all wrong," she declared. "We can sing or walk or ride any time. How often do we get to watch a real cowboy roping demonstration? That was definitely the best thing we did today!"

As her friends continued to bicker over their favourite activities, Emma looked around, hoping to see Jane. But the new girl was nowhere in sight.

Mia noticed her looking. "Don't worry, Emma, you still have the square dancing to do later," she said. "Maybe you can help Jane enjoy that."

"I don't know," Emma said. "She didn't like being the centre of attention when I made her sing that solo. She probably won't want to even try to learn to square dance."

Mia shrugged. "I guess we'll find out."

The five friends spent the rest of the meal talking about other things. Emma kept watching for Jane, but the room was crowded, and she never spotted her.

After a while Cowboy Jack stood up at the front of the room. "Did you all enjoy your meal?" he asked.

Everyone cheered. Stephanie lifted her spoon and fork and clanked them together, while Andrea let out a loud wolf whistle.

Cowboy Jack smiled. "Good. While you were eating, we've been setting up the barn for a good old-fashioned ranch hoedown. I hope you're all ready to square dance!"

"I can't wait," Olivia said to Emma and the others as the rest of the class cheered again. "Maybe we'll get to dance with a real cowboy!"

"If so, I hope he's wearing his boots," Stephanie joked. "Because I've never square danced before – I'll probably step on his toes a few times!" Emma laughed. "You'll do great," she said. "Anyway, none of the rest of us have ever square danced, either. Not even Andrea."

"Right," Andrea agreed. "We don't do square dancing at my dance studio." Her green eyes lit up. "But maybe we should! I might suggest it at my jazz dance lesson next week."

Mia stood up, dropping her napkin on her plate. "Come on, let's get back to the barn."

The five friends hurried out of the dining hall. Emma kept a lookout for Jane on the way, but she didn't see her.

When they arrived in the barn, Emma forgot about Jane for a moment. The place had been transformed! A stage was set up at one end of the large open space, and a band was up there, tuning their instruments. Emma recognized some of the musicians from her earlier activities. Cowboy Jack was holding a microphone. Mrs Marks had an accordion. The young man and woman from the campfire songs activity were tuning their fiddles. The nature walk guide was plucking the strings on a banjo. Eight other employees were standing at the front of the stage.

The women were dressed
in colourful full skirts, while
the men wore dark trousers
and Western shirts with bolo
ties. Emma guessed that they were there to
demonstrate the dance steps.

"OK, everyone," Cowboy Jack called
out. "Grab your partners and let's get ready
to dance!"

"Uh oh." Emma looked around. "I have no
idea where my partner is."

Ms Palmer was standing nearby and heard
her. "It's all right, Emma," she said with a smile.
"You don't need to stick with the same
buddies from earlier. Just find a partner and
join in!"

Emma bit her lip, feeling guilty for
abandoning Jane. But what could she do if the
new girl was nowhere in sight?

Stephanie grabbed her hand. "Come on, Emma," she said. "You can be my partner this time."

"Hey, what about me?" Olivia pretended to pout.

Jacob heard her and bowed in front of her. "May I have this dance?" he asked with a grin.

Olivia blushed. "Of course. Let's go!"

"Everyone have a partner?" Cowboy Jack said into the microphone as the musicians launched into a lively tune. "Good. Now, square dancing requires four couples per group. So divide yourselves up, find an open spot on the floor, and get ready to dance!"

"I'm ready," Jacob called out. "There's just one problem."

"What's that, young cowhand?" Cowboy Jack asked.

Jacob shrugged and grinned. "I have no idea how to square dance."

Cowboy Jack chuckled as everyone laughed. "That's why I'm here. Square dancing is all about doing what the caller – that's me – calls out. We'll be learning different steps and movements, and switching partners a few times along the way. Just listen to me, watch the demonstration dancers, and try to do what they're doing. But really, there's just one unbreakable rule when it comes to square dancing."

"What's that?" Jacob called out.

Cowboy Jack tipped his hat and grinned. "The rule is – you absolutely have to have fun!"

Emma whooped along with everyone else. This was going to be a blast!

9

Dance Partners

"Wow!" Olivia exclaimed breathlessly, collapsing against the wall as the musicians finished yet another song. "Square dancing is harder than it looks!"

Mia giggled, brushing a lock of red hair out of her face. "Definitely," she agreed. "But it's fun!"

Nobody argued with that. The five friends, plus Jacob, had joined with a couple of Jacob's friends to form the required four couples. The eight of them had spent the past forty minutes learning to square dance. Most of the steps were easy, but it was hard to do them as quickly as Cowboy Jack called them out!

"Who wants to be my partner this time?" Stephanie asked.

"Not me!" Andrea exclaimed in mock alarm. "My toes still haven't recovered from the last time."

Stephanie gave her a playful shove. "Come on – I wasn't that bad! At least I didn't elbow you in the ribs like Olivia did to Emma."

Olivia giggled. "Sorry again about that," she said. "I dosied when I was supposed to doe."

"It's OK." Emma smiled at Olivia. "After all, I accidentally pulled your hair when we got tangled up in that turn."

Up on the stage, Cowboy Jack gave a whistle. "Listen up, everyone," he said. "You're all doing great! Keep practising your steps while the musicians take five.

We'll begin
again in
a moment."

"Good," Andrea said. "I need to practise that
swing and promenade thing we did earlier."

She grabbed Mia and twirled her around.
As Emma stepped back out of the way, she
caught a glimpse of black hair nearby. It was Jane!

"Jane's here!" she blurted out in surprise.

"Of course she's here, silly," Stephanie said
with a laugh. "Where else would she go?"

119

"No, look!" Emma pointed. "She's here – with Chelsea!"

Jane and Chelsea were a couple of groups over. The two of them were doing some kind of complicated turn while the rest of their group watched. Jane was laughing as she led Chelsea through the movements.

"Wow," Olivia said, coming over to stand beside Emma. "Jane is really good."

"Yeah. But how in the world did she end up partners with Chelsea?" Stephanie wondered.

"It's my fault." Emma bit her lip. "I ditched her, so she probably got stuck with their group because they needed one more person. I bet she's miserable!"

"I don't know," Olivia said slowly. "She doesn't look miserable."

Stephanie nodded. "She looks like she's having fun."

Emma realized they were right. Jane was still leading her partner through the movements, giggling the entire time. Chelsea looked like she was having fun, too.

"Still, maybe I should check on her," Emma said. "She is supposed to be my buddy for the day."

She hurried over to the other group. Jane and Chelsea stopped dancing when they saw her coming.

"What do you want, Emma?" Chelsea didn't sound very friendly. "Our group is already full."

"I'm not coming to join your group," Emma said. "I just wanted to say hi to Jane. I haven't seen her since our last activity."

"Oh. Um, sorry about that," Jane said. "I ran into Chelsea on the way into dinner and ended up sitting with her."

"You did?" Emma blurted out, astonished. Chelsea was very particular about everything from the brands of designer jeans she wore to the people she hung out with. She wasn't the type of person to invite just anyone to sit with her – especially a shy new girl like Jane.

Chelsea shrugged. "I just wanted to thank her again for saving me from that apple earlier," she told Emma. "I told her with the way she leaped over and grabbed it, she should think about taking up ballet. Especially after I saw her do that jump in the costume place."

"And I told her I've been taking ballet classes since I was four years old," Jane continued with a smile. "Chelsea said she's a dancer, too, and we got to talking, and, well…"

She didn't have to finish; Emma got it. Jane had been so busy chatting with Chelsea that she'd forgotten all about Emma.

"I didn't know you were a ballet dancer, Jane," Emma said, wishing once again that she'd followed Stephanie's advice to ask Jane more questions about herself. "That's cool."

"Not just ballet," Chelsea put in. "She does jazz, tap, contemporary, hip hop – everything! She even took some square dancing lessons at her old studio. She's amazing!"

Jane blushed, but she didn't look embarrassed. She just looked happy. "I'm not that good," she said. "I love to dance, though."

"You'll definitely have to start taking classes with me at Heartlake Dance Studio," Chelsea said. "None of the dancers there are much good other than me, but the teachers are cool."

Emma opened her mouth to remind Chelsea that Andrea danced at the studio, too, and that she was just as good as Chelsea if not better. But she didn't bother. Chelsea and Jane were already spinning off into another circle. Besides, Emma could see Cowboy Jack picking up the microphone. She needed to get back to her friends.

"Um, OK," she called to Jane. "Have fun."

"Don't worry," Chelsea called back as she and Jane swung past. "We will."

10
Perfect Match

"That was fun, wasn't it?" Andrea said as she settled back beside Emma. The bus had just turned out of the Sunshine Ranch's long drive and was trundling down the highway towards Heartlake City. It was late, and the bus was dark except for the faint glow of the safety lights and the light of the half moon peeking in through the windows.

Stephanie looked over the back of the seat in front of Emma and Andrea. "Definitely the best class trip yet!" she declared.

"Square dancing was fun, wasn't it?" Mia said

with a yawn as she kneeled on the seat beside Stephanie. "It was tiring, though."

Emma nodded. She never would have guessed she'd get to try so many new things in one day! The campfire songs had been fun, at least until she'd tricked Jane into singing that solo. The Western riding had been great, too. It was just too bad that Jane was so allergic to horses that she couldn't try it. Picking apples had been a little stressful, since it had turned out that neither Emma nor Jane enjoyed the logical approach to an activity like that. But the apples themselves had been delicious, and Emma couldn't wait to ask her parents to drive out to the ranch next weekend and buy some. Then there had been the cowboy costumes, the nature walk, and the roping show. And of course, the delicious cowboy feast followed by the evening of square dancing.

Emma glanced towards the back of the bus. Chelsea was sitting there again – only this time, she and her snobby friends had made way for one more person: Jane.

"Do you think Chelsea really wants to be friends with Jane?" Emma asked the others worriedly. "What if she's just acting nice so she can tease her? Chelsea can be kind of mean like that sometimes."

"Yeah, she can." Mia shrugged and glanced back at Jane and the others. "I don't think this is one of those times, though."

Andrea nodded. "She really seems to like Jane."

"Jane seems to like her, too," Stephanie added. "Weird!"

"Definitely weird." Emma chewed her lower lip.

She still couldn't believe how quickly the two girls had hit it off. She never would have predicted it!

Olivia leaned towards Emma. She was sitting across the aisle with a girl from the science club. "Don't worry about it, Emma," Olivia said kindly. "The important thing is that Jane found a friend."

"I guess." Emma frowned slightly. "But isn't it kind of strange that the friend she found is Chelsea?"

"Yes and no," Stephanie said. "Maybe Chelsea isn't the friend any of us would've picked for her. But friendship can't be forced. And it isn't always logical."

Mia smiled. "Right," she said. "I know Jane and Chelsea are total opposites in some ways."

"Jane is quiet, and Chelsea talks way too much – mostly about herself," Stephanie added.

Andrea laughed. "Jane hates being the centre of attention unless she's dancing, and Chelsea loves having all eyes on her no matter what she's doing."

"But obviously they have something important in common – they both love dancing," Mia said. "That's what brought them together."

"Just like chasing down Olivia's rascally puppy brought the five of us together," Stephanie put in.

Olivia nodded. "I mean, look at us, Emma," she said. "We're all super different in a whole lot of ways. You're a dreamy artist, I'm a logical scientist, Steph is really organized, Andrea lives to perform, and Mia is obsessed with animals."

"But we all have stuff in common, too," Emma continued, finally getting it. "We support each other, and we just plain like each other. And that's why our friendship works so well despite our differences."

Stephanie grinned. "Exactly!"

Emma glanced at Jane again. The new girl was whispering with Chelsea, their heads so close that Jane's dark hair mixed with Chelsea's blonde locks. Both girls looked happy.

"OK," Emma said, her worries lifting. "Does that mean my makeover was a success after all?"

Andrea giggled. "Not exactly," she said. "All you did was drive Jane crazy so she ended up running off with Chelsea."

"But that still counts," Olivia argued. "After all, it worked, Jane isn't lonely any more."

Emma thought about that. "You know, maybe Jane didn't need a makeover after all," she mused. "She just needed a chance to be herself. And to find someone who likes her for who she is. No makeover required."

"Good point," Mia said. "During the roping demonstration, one of the cowboys said there's a perfect horse for every cowpoke. Maybe there's a perfect best friend for every girl, too."

"Or four," Andrea put in, winking at Emma and the others.

"Right," Emma agreed. "Like Steph said before, maybe Chelsea isn't the best friend I would have picked out for Jane. But she's the one Jane chose for herself. And I'm really glad they found each other. I hope they have as much fun together as the five of us always do." She threw an arm around Andrea and smiled at the others.

THE END

HORSES, HORSES, HORSES!

The LEGO® Friends all LOVE horses!
Learn more about the ones the girls
met at the Sunshine Ranch:

Blaize

Curious and sweet, Blaize gets his name from the
big white blaze running down his nose. He's a white
Welsh Pony, and always likes to stick his nose – blaze
and all! – into everything that goes on at the ranch.
He's well trained and easy to ride, and everyone who
visits loves taking him out for a trot across the fields.

Mocca

Mocca is the biggest horse on the ranch. She's a
Belgian, which is a breed of draft horse. In the
winter, she even pulls a sleigh! She might be large,
but she's also very gentle and calm, which makes
her perfect for teaching beginners to ride.

Fame

The newest addition to the Sunshine Ranch, Fame is
Mocca's foal. He's a pretty palomino with a spunky
attitude. Mia was there when he was born – her
grandparents called her as soon as they could tell that
Mocca was ready to have her baby. It was one
of the most special moments of Mia's
life, and Fame will always be very
special to her.

HORSEY TRIVIA

Horses can sleep standing up – they lock their leg muscles so they won't fall over. They only need to sleep for around two to three hours per day.

Newborn foals can usually stand within an hour of being born, and they can run within a day.

Horses' eyes are larger than those of any other land mammal. Because their eyes are on the sides of their heads, they can see almost all the way around themselves.

Horses' teeth never stop growing. You can estimate a horse's age by its teeth.

Horses do neigh, nicker, and whinny, but not nearly as much as they do in the movies. Most of their communication is through body language.

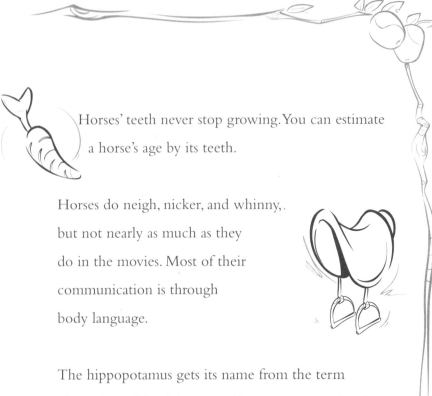

The hippopotamus gets its name from the term "river horse" but hippos and horses are not related at all. Most people probably don't want to try riding a hippopotamus, either – although Mia might be game!

COUNTRY AND WESTERN STYLE

If you want to fit in on the ranch, Emma has a few tips for you on how to look like a real cowgirl:

First, pair a denim skirt or jeans with a white vest.

Pick out a cute checked or floral buttoned shirt, ideally with some fringe, and tie the tails in a knot at your waist.

Layer on a suede vest or embroidered jacket – and again, look for one with fringe if you can!

Top it all off with a pair of cowboy boots, an oversized belt buckle, and of course a cowgirl hat!

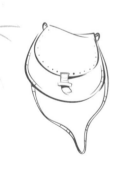

Now you're ready to ride the range in style! But the most important thing is your cowgirl attitude – don't be afraid to jump right into any activity and get your hands dirty!

OVERCOMING SHYNESS

Emma noticed that Jane was shy and wanted to find ways to help her. Being shy isn't a crime, but it can keep you from having fun and meeting new people. If you find yourself feeling nervous when faced with a new situation, try some of these tips:

Spend time with people who make you feel comfortable. Ask them to help you meet others.

♥ ♥ ♥

Whenever you feel nervous, take long, deep breaths to help yourself relax.

If you start to compare yourself to others and worry that you don't measure up, take a moment to remind yourself of all your best qualities – your sense of humour, a great smile, a love for animals, loyalty to your 'friends . . . or' whatever it is that makes YOU special.

Be prepared – if you're nervous about giving a presentation in class or performing in public, make sure you practise ahead of time. That will help you feel more confident.

Don't try to overcome your shyness all at once, or you may become overwhelmed and give up. Do a little at a time, and before you know it, you'll be the life of the party!

TRIP TIPS

Is your class going on a school trip soon? If so, take these helpful hints from the LEGO Friends about how to make the most of it.

Emma says: Dress for success – make sure to match your clothes and shoes to the day's planned activities.

Andrea says:
Pack plenty of snacks and entertainment for the bus ride. Don't forget your mp3 player!

Stephanie says: Bring a camera (or the camera on your mobile phone) to record all the fun moments you'll want to share and remember.

Olivia says: Have fun with your friends – but also take the time to get to know some of your other classmates better.

Mia says: Most important of all – have fun and make the most of the special day!

IMPRESSIONS:

MIA: It turns out that Western riding isn't THAT different from English riding – but it was a lot of fun anyway! Can't wait to do it again soon!

OLIVIA: I'm all about new tech, but doing stuff the old fashioned way is cool, too – like picking apples, etc. at the Sunshine Ranch! Can't wait 2 go back!

ANDREA: Now I'm totally ready if I ever get cast as a cowgirl in a movie. I just hope the director decides to film at the Sunshine Ranch!

STEPHANIE: I could write a ten-page article for the school paper about our trip – and I probably will! For now, I'll describe it in one word: FUN!

EMMA: The Sunshine Ranch taught me lots about Western riding, apple picking, etc. But mostly it reminded me of the power of friendship.
LUV MY BFFS!!!